Noddy the Rainbow Chaser

HarperCollins *Children's Books*

It was a special day in Toy Town. A magic rainbow was sparkling in the sky over Town Square. Everyone was very excited.

"It's so beautiful!" cried Tessie Bear. "Look at
the yellow."

"Look at the orange," mewed Miss Pink Cat.

"And this red!" said Mr Wobbly Man.

"I love all the colours!" smiled Noddy. "But it
hasn't rained. So where has this rainbow come from?"

"It's a magic rainbow, Noddy," said Big-Ears.
"So it doesn't need rain. It just turns up when
it feels like it."

"And makes everyone happy," added
Miss Pink Cat. "I know, because it's been
coming ever since I was a Pink Kitten!"

Just then, the naughty goblins arrived. "Huh!
Happy!" sneered Gobbo. "Who cares? There's
a big pot of gold at the end of that rainbow."

"And when we find it WE'LL be happy!" said Sly.
"Cos we'll be RICH!"

"Oh, no you won't!" said Mr Plod. "Because you're going to the police station, right now. Miss Pink Cat tells me you've been after her pies again!" And he whisked the grumbling goblins away.

Noddy looked thoughtful.

"Oh, Noddy!" said Master Tubby Bear. "Do you really believe that story about the pot of gold?"

"Come with me, Tubby Bear," grinned Noddy. "I've just had a brilliant idea!"

Noddy took Master Tubby Bear to find the
Toy Town plane.

"The goblins were right about one thing.
It WOULD be nice to have all that gold,"
said Tubby Bear.

"That's why we're going on a treasure hunt
– at the end of the magic rainbow!" said Noddy.

And Noddy sang a song:

Each of us would have a golden house
'Neath a silver tree.
What great fun for you and me
To be as rich as rich can be.

"So what are we waiting for? Let's follow that rainbow!"

It didn't take the friends long to get ready and soon they were in the air.

"I can't WAIT to get that treasure," sighed Master Tubby Bear, happily.

But then Noddy saw where the rainbow was leading them… To the Dark Wood!

"Maybe I don't want that gold, after all,"
said Master Tubby Bear.

But Noddy wouldn't give up so easily.
He landed the plane right in the middle
of Dark Wood!

"Follow me!" said Noddy, bravely.

Shimmering in the darkness, the magic rainbow stretched straight ahead. But fierce eyes winked at them through the gloom.

"I don't like this ONE BIT," grumbled Master Tubby Bear, running after his friend.

Suddenly, there it was. The end of the rainbow. And there, on top of a hillock was a pot full of glittering GOLD!

"WE'VE FOUND THE TREASURE!" yelled Noddy.

And the friends did a little dance for joy.

But then Noddy had a scary thought.
"Wait! Maybe there is a magic spell
protecting the pot of gold. We'd better
watch out!" he said.

All of a sudden, Tubby Bear felt someone tap him on the back.

"Is that you behind me, Noddy?" he quavered.

"I'm IN FRONT of you," said Noddy. "How can it be me?"

Poor Master Tubby Bear. The trees were coming
alive. A long branch snatched him up and he
was dangling in the air!

"Get me down!" yelled Tubby Bear.

Noddy jumped up as high as he could and grabbed
hold of Tubby Bear's shoes. Then he pulled and he
pulled and he PULLED!

"He-e-elp!" squeaked Master Tubby Bear,
as he slipped out of the grasp of the magic tree.

Noddy and Master Tubby Bear fell to the ground
and tumbled over and over.

"Whew!" said Noddy. "That was close!"

But they weren't safe yet.

The magic spell hadn't finished.

A magic storm whistled through the trees
and whirled them up into the air.

Round and round they tossed until the wind
blew them back into Noddy's plane.

"Now I AM giving up," said Noddy. "Let's
go home!"

"But the treasure's just underneath us, Noddy,"
said Master Tubby Bear.

Noddy looked down from his plane and a very
daring idea came into his head.

"Let's SCOOP it up, then. With the plane!"

Noddy was a good pilot and he held the plane steady as it roared over the Dark Wood.

Closer and closer they got to the pot of gold until Master Tubby Bear could drop a rope to grab hold of it.

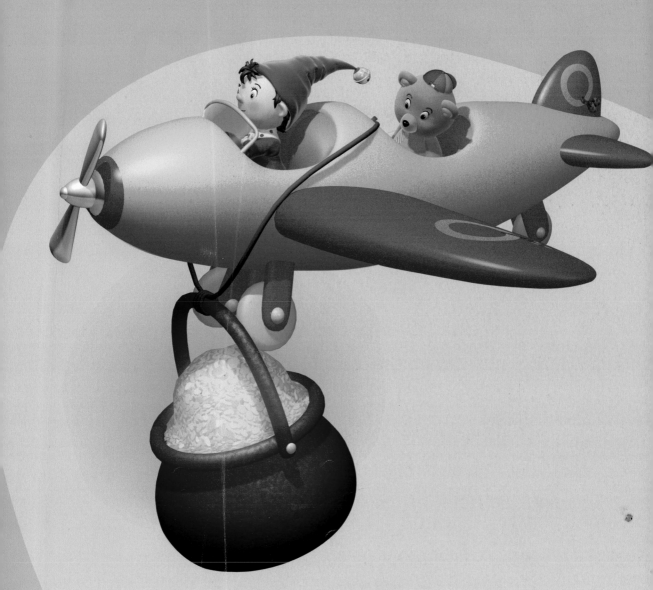

"We've GOT THE GOLD!" whooped Noddy. Then,
all of a sudden, the magic rainbow disappeared.
   "Where did it go?" asked Master Tubby Bear.
   "I don't know," said Noddy. "But one thing
I DO know. Everyone is going to be very happy
with us back in Toy Town!"

Everyone thought Noddy and Master Tubby Bear
had been so brave.

"They're heroes!" cried Miss Pink Cat.
Noddy smiled proudly, but Big-Ears frowned.

"Did the rainbow disappear when you took the
pot of gold?" he asked.

Noddy nodded.

"Oh, dear!" said Big-Ears sadly. "That gold was put there by magic. It's what made the rainbow sparkle. Now it has been taken away, our wonderful rainbow has vanished for ever."

It was as if a big grey cloud had settled on Toy Town.

Everyone felt terrible.

"Oh, no!" sniffed Tessie Bear. "I loved all those beautiful colours!"

"So did I," sighed Mr Wobbly Man.

"Don't be SAD!" cried Noddy. "I'll buy everyone an ice-cream!"

"I just want our rainbow back," said Tessie Bear.

"Oh, Big-Ears!" cried Noddy. "What can I do?"

"There is one thing you can do," said Big-Ears and he whispered in Noddy's ear.

Soon afterwards, Noddy and Tubby Bear were in the plane again – only this time, they were taking the pot of gold BACK to the Dark Wood.

The second that the pot hit the ground, the magic rainbow sprang back into the air, sparkling more brightly than ever over Toy Town.

"We've done it, Tubby Bear," laughed Noddy
and now I think we both deserve an ice-cream,
don't you?"
    And Master Tubby Bear had to agree.

First published in Great Britain by HarperCollins Publishers Ltd in 2003
This edition published by HarperCollins Children's Books
HarperCollins Children's Books is a division of HarperCollins Publishers Ltd.

Text and images copyright © 2003 Enid Blyton Ltd (a Chorion company).
The word "NODDY" is a registered trade mark of Enid Blyton Ltd. All rights reserved.
For further information on Noddy please contact www.NODDY.com

ISBN-10: 0-00-778461-9
ISBN-13: 978-0-00-778461-5

A CIP catalogue for this title is available from the British Library.
All rights reserved. No part of this publication may be reproduced, stored in a retrieval system or transmitted
in any form or by any means, electronic, mechanical, photocopying, recording or otherwise, without the prior
permission of HarperCollins Publishers Ltd,
77-85 Fulham Palace Rd, Hammersmith, London, W6 8JB.

Visit our website at: www.harpercollinschildrensbooks.co.uk

Printed and bound by Printing Express Ltd, Hong Kong